My Father, the Enemy

My Father, the Enemy

Michael J. Pellowski

Art by Stan Goldberg

Hollywood Paperbacks

FIRST EDITION
1 3 5 7 9 10 8 6 4 2

Library of Congress Cataloging-in-Publication Data
Pellowski, Michael.
    My father, the enemy/Michael J. Pellowski —1st ed.
      p. cm.—(Riverdale High; #8)
    Summary: Veronica battles her father over the
construction of a mall that would destroy
an old growth forest in Riverdale.
ISBN 1-56282-189-X
    [1. Old growth forests—Fiction. 2. Forests and
forestry—Fiction. 3. Conservation of natural
resources—Fiction. 4. Environmental protection—
Fiction. 5. Fathers and daughters—Fiction.]
I. Title. II. Series: Pellowski, Michael. Riverdale
High; #8.
PZ7.P3656Mu 1992
[Fic]—dc20 91-58615 CIP AC

My Father, the Enemy

Other titles in the Riverdale High series

Chapter 1

"I still think we should have brought a basket lunch with us," Jughead grumbled. He slumped between Betty Cooper and Reggie Mantle in the backseat of Archie Andrews's beat-up bright red jalopy. I turned to glare at Juggie as Ol' Betsy, Archie's wreck on wheels, sputtered, rattled, and bounced its way down a country lane.

"Jughead Jones, quit complaining," I snapped. "All you've done for the past twenty minutes is gripe about food!" I gave Jug an icy glare. "We told you when we left Pop Tate's soda shop back in Riverdale that our first trip to Evergreen Forest this summer was for a nature walk, not a picnic!"

"Ronnie's right," Archie chimed in, peeking at Jug in the rearview mirror.

"And if I remember correctly, you invited yourself along. So quit grousing."

Jughead took a deep breath and exhaled loudly. "What is this—pick-on-Jughead-Jones day?" he muttered. "I make a few simple remarks and Miss Veronica 'Touchy' Lodge jumps down my throat." Jug turned to stare at the back of Archie's neck. "And you'd think at least my best buddy would stick up for me," he added. Jug and Archie had been best pals since grammar school.

"How can I stick up for you when everything Ron said is true?" Archie answered without taking his eyes off the road. In spite of Archie's careful attention, Ol' Betsy seemed to be hitting every pothole in sight. "We made it perfectly clear to you that this wasn't going to be a picnic."

"Hmph!" grunted Jug. He slouched even farther down in his seat. "When Ron said you guys weren't taking any food with you, I thought you were just trying to keep me from tagging along." He folded his arms across his chest. "I figured Betty had a few of her delicious homemade sub sandwiches stashed in the car somewhere or that Ronnie had had her chef prepare some kind of snack. How was I supposed to know you guys weren't fooling?"

I looked back at Betty and rolled my eyes. Betty just shrugged. Figuring out Jughead's weird logic was totally impossible. In fact, the only predictable thing about Juggie was his insatiable appetite. He loved food as much as Reggie loved pulling practical jokes.

"This is going to be a great nature walk," Reg commented sarcastically. "Before it's finished, old Needlenose will be gnawing on tree bark to satisfy his craving for something to eat."

Jug shot Reg a wicked look.

"Don't be so hard on Juggie, Reg," Betty scolded. "He can't help it if he has to eat constantly. It's his metabolism. Look how thin he is."

I wasn't surprised Betty had jumped to Jughead's defense. It was typical of her. At the end of the school year, just before summer vacation, Betty had been voted Everybody's Pal in the Riverdale Yearbook Poll. She had been my best friend for years.

"Betty is right," grunted Jud. "I have an ultra-active metabolism." He patted his stomach. It rumbled so loud that even the noise of Ol' Betsy's sputtering engine didn't drown it out.

"Oh, for heaven's sake," I exclaimed, reaching for my purse. I quickly searched through its contents and pulled out a thick Swiss chocolate bar I'd put in there the day before. "Here," I said to Jughead as I tossed the candy into his lap. "Maybe this will tide you over."

Jug's eyes lit up like 100-watt bulbs. "Thanks, Ron," he said. "You're an angel of mercy." He hurriedly peeled the paper off and took a big bite of the candy. "Yum," he sighed contentedly. "I love imported chocolate." He chewed and swallowed, then added, "But I still wish someone had brought along a picnic basket."

I spun back around in the front seat to face the road. "It's hopeless," I moaned to Archie.

"Forget Jug," Archie advised. "Just think about the quiet serenity of Evergreen Forest. It's beautiful this time of year."

"It's beautiful all year long," I replied. I remembered when I'd first moved to Riverdale, I'd had trouble making friends be-

4

cause I was a new kid and rich, to boot. I'd ride out here on my bike, and I'd take long walks and sort of talk to the trees. It made me feel less lonely. Since then, I've always considered this place more of a friend than a forest.

The dirt road turnoff that led to the forest wasn't much farther. "Evergreen Forest is one of the few unspoiled wilderness areas left around Riverdale," Archie commented. "And it's one of the only old-growth forests in the state. Some of the trees are more than a hundred years old."

"Thanks for the science lesson," Reggie remarked dryly. He shifted his weight around in the backseat. "That's just what I need—to be reminded of school during summer vacation."

We all ignored Reggie's comment. Ignoring Reggie was sort of a rule of thumb around Riverdale High. Reggie never seemed to mind. As class clown, he didn't really expect to be taken too seriously.

"There's the old road," Archie said. He made a sharp turn onto the narrow dirt lane that led to Evergreen Forest through the back. Actually, the forest didn't have an official name. As kids, we'd simply dubbed it Evergreen Forest because of all of the pine, spruce, and cedar trees that grew there.

"Here we are at last," Archie announced. He pulled Ol' Betsy off the path, onto a small, grassy clearing. When he turned the key to the off position, Ol' Betsy sputtered, coughed, and wheezed. *Kapow!* The car backfired loudly and then shook so violently that my teeth rattled. Finally the engine stopped running and the car became motionless.

"I guess I need a tune-up," Archie said, opening the door on his side of the car.

"What you need is a new car," Reggie retorted. He stood up and stretched.

"Oh, yeah?" Archie really loved Ol' Betsy and was very defensive about her. He turned angrily to face Reggie while he tried to climb out. He caught his foot on the seat and tumbled out headfirst onto the grass. He ended up flat on his back.

"Are you okay, Archiekins?" I called, as Betty and I raced to his side.

"Ah, sure," Archie said in embarrassment. "I meant to do that."

"Right," chuckled Reggie. He got out and joined us. "Now old Orangehead is practicing to be a stuntman." Reggie stared down at Archie, still sprawled on the turf. "You didn't fracture any of your freckles, did you?"

"No!" Archie answered indignantly. "But I could use a hand up."

"*I* could use another candy bar," Jughead muttered, coming over to join the rest of us. Jug and Reggie pulled Archie to his feet.

I sneaked a peek at Betty and we smiled at each other. Wherever Archie went, he was plagued by all sorts of minor mishaps. Archie is sweet, considerate, and handsome, but he can sure be clumsy sometimes.

"Let's get going," Archie said, pocketing his car keys and dusting himself off.

"Lead on, Scout," Jughead joked. He snapped to attention and saluted so stiffly that he almost knocked his trademark hat off his head.

"This way," Archie directed. We followed him into the shadowy forest, slowly snaking our way around the huge trunks of towering oaks and elms. Here and there the gigantic hardwoods shared space and light with tightly packed clusters of massive conifers. Before long we were deep in the woods, enjoying the melodious sounds of birds calling to each other from distant treetops. Suddenly the serenity of the remote wildlife area was shattered by a loud, rumbling sound. We all froze in our tracks.

"Don't look at me," Jughead said, putting his hands across his midsection.

"What is that?" Archie asked as the noise grew.

"It's coming from that direction," I said. I pointed to our left, beyond a thick blind of fir trees.

"Maybe it's a farmer doing some work," Betty suggested.

"There are nothing but pastures and meadows around these woods," Archie reminded us. "And it's all state land."

"Let's investigate," Reggie proposed.

For once we didn't ignore him. We moved toward the curtain of evergreen trees that hid the source of the disturbing sounds. It was very slow progress through the thick trees.

I was starting to get a bit angry. Tramping through thick underbrush wasn't exactly my idea of fun. Our nature walk was turning into a survival test. "My hair is getting totally ruined," I grunted, ducking under a low branch. "Whatever we find better be worth all this aggravation." I

wanted to find out what was making that racket as much as everyone else, but not at the cost of looking like a backwoods ragamuffin.

"Look!" Jug exclaimed as my friends emerged into a vast meadow. "Can you believe it?"

"What is it?" I asked. I pushed aside some spruce branches and stepped out so I could see.

"It's a construction crew," Archie replied.

We all stood like statues at the edge of the meadow, gaping at a bulldozer, a construction trailer, and several pickup trucks. The bulldozer was clearing a section of the meadow where the dirt road ended. That was the source of the rumbling we'd heard. Around the trailer, men in hard hats were crouched over a portable table. They were studying blueprints. Other workers were hammering a huge wooden sign to a tree.

"They can't be building something way out here," Betty mumbled in disbelief.

"Well, they're not here for a picnic," Reggie said.

"Let's find out what this is all about," Archie urged. He waved us forward. We walked up to the sign the men had just put up and stared at the neatly printed words.

"Future Home of the New Riverdale Industrial Park," I read out loud. I looked at my friends. "I don't like the sound of that."

"Neither do I," Archie and Betty replied together. As we stood there staring open-mouthed at the sign, a man walked up to us. I guess he was an engineer.

"Can I help you kids?" he asked, flashing us a phony smile.

Archie nodded. "We were wondering what this sign means."

The man shrugged his shoulders. "It means just what it says," he replied politely. "We're putting up an industrial park here, and it's going to be quite a project." The thought seemed to please him. "In addition to a half dozen warehouses, there are going to be at least three major companies setting up shop in this new complex."

Reggie whistled.

"But how can you fit all of that in this one meadow?" Betty asked innocently.

The man laughed. "We can't, miss!" he answered. He pointed at the woods from which we'd just emerged. "All of that is going. It's going to be cleared for industrial development."

"What?" I cried. "Evergreen Forest? *No!* You can't!" Losing the forest would be like watching a friend die.

"We sure can," the man said. "And we will. It's already a done deal."

"B-but this is public land," Archie argued.

The man shook his head. "Not anymore it isn't," he corrected. "Riverdale's planning and zoning board have already made the necessary changes to allow us to purchase and clear this parcel." The man paused for a minute. "Riverdale's sagging economy really needs the financial boost this industrial park will provide."

"I know there are people in Riverdale who need work, but we need this forest more," Betty pleaded. "You can't bulldoze those trees."

The man looked at Betty and shrugged. "Like I said, miss," he replied, "it's a done deal. Title to this land has already been transferred. In fact, technically you're all trespassing."

I didn't like the way the man said that.

He had started out friendly enough, but now he was getting a bit arrogant.

"Just a minute," I said. "We didn't see any No Trespassing signs."

"That's right," Reggie backed me up.

"They'll be up soon," the man answered. "So if I were you kids, I wouldn't bother coming back here anymore. This forest will be nothing but a memory by the time winter gets here." He grinned in a plastic way. "Now I have to get back to work." He walked away.

"I can't believe they're going to bulldoze Evergreen Forest to build an industrial park," Betty groaned. "It's . . . it's a crime against nature!" She looked back at the trees behind us and shook her head. She didn't know what else to say.

"It figures," Reggie said as we started back. "Some greedy, money-grubbing businessman must stand to make a bundle by ruining our forest. He's probably some lousy creep who lives in a big city and doesn't care one bit about the people in Riverdale."

"Yeah," Jug agreed. "The only thing green a louse like that cares about is money."

"We shouldn't take this lying down,"

13

Archie proclaimed. "Somebody's got to stop this."

"You're right, Archie," I agreed. "If money is the only thing people like this developer understands, then we'll fight with money." I was really ticked off. I didn't like the way the man at the sign had talked to us, and I wouldn't stand by while Evergreen Forest was destroyed. Evergreen Forest was a friend of mine— as much a friend as Betty—and I always stood up for my friends. I wasn't about to let some outsider come in and tear down my forest. "My father will back us on this," I vowed to my friends. "He's a defender of the environment. Just last month he contributed ten thousand dollars to the Save the Tropical Rainforest Fund." My father, Hiram Lodge, was Riverdale's richest man.

"All right!" Archie cheered. "If Mr. Lodge gets involved in this, you know people will stand up and listen."

Betty smiled and nodded. "They sure will. But first we've got to find out who we're fighting against."

"How do we do that?" Reggie asked as we continued walking through the forest.

"We can find out by going to the plan-

14

ning board," Betty answered. Betty always seemed to know just what to do. "They'll have the name of the developer on file, and it's a matter of public record."

"Well, let's go, then!" I said defiantly. "The Lodges are not going to stand idly by while Evergreen Forest is turned into a parking lot."

Archie looked at me with admiration in his eyes. It made me feel proud of myself. I was determined to fight for Evergreen Forest.

Chapter 2

All the way back to Riverdale we hatched plots to terminate the proposed industrial park. Of course most of our ideas were too farfetched to be of any real use. For example, Reggie proposed a Rambo-type approach that included capturing the engineer's trailer and then sabotaging all of the heavy equipment.

"Like, get real, Reg," I said—even though we all knew he was just blowing smoke.

"We could write to our representatives in Congress," Betty suggested.

"Hmph," Jug grunted. "By the time we'd get a response, Evergreen Forest would be kindling. Anyway, since we're not old enough to vote yet, our concerns don't carry much weight with elected officials."

"Jug is right," Archie agreed. "Our only hope is Mr. Lodge." He glanced at me and I smiled confidently.

"Don't worry," I assured my friends. "Daddykins won't let us down. When he hears what's going on, he'll charge to the rescue of Evergreen Forest like a knight in shining armor."

"I'm sure my parents will help, too," Archie said. "My dad often speaks of Evergreen Forest. He and Reggie's dad used to camp there when they were young." Archie glanced at Reggie.

"I still say we should storm the trailer," said Reggie. Obviously he'd been watching too many movies lately.

"Give it a rest, dude," Jughead snapped.

I was surprised at how concerned Juggie seemed to be about the destruction of the forest. He hadn't mentioned food or eating at all since we'd left the construction site. For once something had taken priority over his appetite.

Jug looked at Archie. "I'm sure all our parents will stand up for this cause." He glanced at Betty and Reg. They both nodded. "But we need a strong leader to guide our actions, and that's why we need Mr. Lodge. He knows all the right people and he knows how to get things done."

"Speaking of getting things done," said Archie as we approached the Riverdale Municipal Building, "let's find out who's behind this scheme to rob Riverdale of a natural treasure." Archie pulled Ol' Betsy into the parking lot. If I didn't know it was impossible, I'd swear that even Ol' Betsy was on our side. She had gotten us from the forest to the lot without stalling a single time—a record.

"It's this way," Betty informed us as she marched toward the door. We went into the building and quickly made our way to the right department. Betty had once been Mayor for a Day as part of a student government-awareness program, so she knew the building well. "In here," Betty announced as we came to a halt in front of a door inscribed Planning and Zoning.

I felt it was my turn now to take the initiative. "Okay, troops," I commanded, "charge!" I pushed the door open and we burst into the reception area like police on a raid.

"Now what's all this?" the secretary seated behind the reception desk asked curtly as our advance stalled before her.

"Ah, we want some information about a proposed industrial park," I said forcefully, after a stuttering start.

"That's right!" Reggie added. He pushed to the front of our pack.

"Is that so?" the secretary replied in a tone that was so cold it practically dripped ice.

"Yes, ma'am," said Archie politely. He smiled disarmingly, but his charm had no effect on the lady.

"I'm sorry, but I don't have the time to answer questions for a bunch of misguided teenagers all hopped up about some industrial this or that," she snapped.

"But this is important," Betty pleaded. "And we're entitled to the information. It's a matter of public record."

I glanced at Betty. I guess if I put as much time into doing homework and reports as she did, I'd know stuff like that, too. Then again, I was a much better shopper than Betty was. And I knew how to deal with crabby salespeople. I was certain the same approach would work with the secretary.

"Who is in charge around here?" I demanded as the secretary began to turn her back to us. Slowly the woman faced me.

"Mr. Slattery is the chairman of the planning board," she replied. Her eyes fired daggers in my direction. I couldn't guess why she was being so rude. Maybe she thought we were there to pester her, or maybe she just didn't like teenagers.

"Is Mr. Slattery in?" I asked. I looked at the doors behind her, searching for an indication as to which office was Slattery's. It was the one just to the left of the secretary's desk. Mr. Slattery's name was on the door and it was open a crack.

"Mr. Slattery is in, but you can't see him," the secretary answered stubbornly. "What is this in reference to again?"

This time Jughead spoke up. "It's about an industrial park scheduled to be built outside of Riverdale at a place we call Evergreen Forest," he said. "Do you know the place we're talking about?"

"Evergreen Forest," mused the woman, stroking her chin thoughtfully. "Do you mean the wooded area off the highway, with those really tall trees?"

I rolled my eyes. I heard Jug exhale impatiently. "Yes!" he said.

"That's the site of the new Riverdale industrial park," she replied. We were back to square one. "That's old news. There was a small piece about it in the paper a while ago. Construction is set to begin this month. It's the biggest project this office has coordinated in years."

I glanced at Archie. "This is getting us nowhere," I said angrily. I started toward Mr. Slattery's office. "We want to see Mr. Slattery right now," I demanded.

The secretary rushed out from behind her desk to block my path. "Wait a minute, miss," she snapped. "Stop! Just who do you think you are?"

I halted and stared her right in the eye. "I'm Veronica Lodge, the daughter of Hiram Lodge," I said in a loud voice. "And I want to see Mr. Slattery this instant!"

There was a brief second of silence. Then we heard a voice from Mr. Slattery's office. "Veronica Lodge?" a man said with a twinge of recognition in his voice. I looked back at my friends and winked. "Hiram Lodge's daughter?" We heard footsteps approach the door. The door opened. A middle-aged man with a receding hairline and thick glasses peered out at me. He adjusted his tie with one hand and pointed at me with his other hand. "Are you Hiram Lodge's daughter?" he asked.

"Yes, I am," I stated proudly. I pushed past the stunned secretary.

"It's all right, Ms. Watkins," the man said, dismissing the secretary. "I'll speak to these youngsters." My friends moved up closer behind me. "I'm Mr. Slattery," he announced. "What can I do for you?"

"We just found out that an industrial complex is going to be built on a stretch of public land we call Evergreen Forest," I told Mr. Slattery. "The complex is known as Riverdale Industrial Park. We want to know what company or person is building that mall."

Mr. Slattery looked at me and blinked rapidly. "Don't you know?" he asked, as if the answer should have been obvious to me.

"Of course not!" I fired back. "If I did, I wouldn't be asking you, would I?"

Mr. Slattery shook his head. "Well, you *should* know," he answered. "The park is being developed by H. L. International Development Corporation."

My eyes widened in shock. My vision blurred for an instant. I was too stunned to do or say anything. It was no wonder Mr. Slattery had rushed out to greet me when he heard who I was. I guess I started to wobble then, because Archie came up to support me.

"Ronnie? Ronnie? Are you okay?" he asked.

I got myself together, broke free of Archie's grasp, and turned toward the door. Without so much as a good-bye to Mr. Slattery, I stepped toward the exit.

"What is it, Ronnie?" Betty asked as I passed her. "Where are you going?"

"I'm going home," I said. My confused friends fell in behind me. They followed me out of the office and into the hall.

"Going home?" sputtered Reggie. "For what?"

"For a snack?" Jug said hopefully. His appetite had finally returned.

"To talk to my father," I grunted angrily, storming toward the exit.

"What's this all about?" Archie persisted as we left the building and headed for his car. "Why are you so ticked off all of a sudden? Do you know something about this H. L. International Development Corporation?"

I stopped dead in my tracks and faced my friends. "H. L. International Development Corporation is one of my father's companies," I confessed. "H. L. stands for 'Hiram Lodge'!"

Chapter 3

It was a short but tension-charged ride to my family's estate. What could anyone say? I'd bragged about how much help my father would be, and now he had turned out to be the cause of the problem. I couldn't believe it! My own father was willing to sacrifice a beautiful place like Evergreen Forest just to make more money. I was angry, hurt, and disappointed. How could he do it? How could he? I had to have an answer—*now*.

"Ah, do you want us to leave?" Archie asked as he stopped Ol' Betsy in front of my house.

I shook my head.

"Well, maybe it would be better if we wait out here while you talk to your dad," Betty said. She smiled at me weakly.

"I think my father owes us all an explanation," I replied. I was having a tough time keeping my temper under control. I got out of Ol' Betsy and slammed the door shut. "I want you all to come with me."

Archie glanced at Betty and Reggie and then switched off the car's engine. It sputtered and died with a loud backfire. Everyone clambered out as I stormed up to the front door. Before I could touch the latch, the door was pulled open by Smithers, our butler.

"Hello, Miss Veronica," he greeted, holding the door for my friends. "I saw you coming up the walk."

"Thank you, Smithers," I answered gruffly. "Where is my father?"

"He's in the den, Miss," Smithers answered. He closed the door behind Jughead, who was the last to enter the house.

"Come on," I urged, stomping off toward my dad's den. My friends followed. When we reached the den, we found the heavy oak door shut. I curled my fingers into a fist and rapped on the wood with all of my might. "Daddykins! I need to speak to you right now," I bellowed at the top of my lungs.

"Well don't break the door down," my father answered. "Come in."

I shoved the door open and charged into the room, followed by my four friends. My father was behind his huge desk. He had a phone in his hand, and he was just placing it back on its cradle. I stepped up to my father's desk. Archie, Jug, Betty, and Reg crowded in around me.

"Is there some connection between the murderous looks on your faces and your visit with Mr. Slattery at the planning board?" my father asked before I could utter a sound. "Now I know how a convict must feel when he comes face-to-face with a lynch mob."

"Sorry, Mr. Lodge," Archie apologized. "We didn't mean to—"

"Oh yes we did!" I said, cutting Archie off in midsentence. I glared at my father. "How did you find out about our visit to the planning board?"

My father pointed to the phone. "Mr. Slattery called me," he explained. "The way you bolted out of his office upset him. He was worried about you." Daddykins rose out of his chair and sat on his desk. "I told him not to be concerned. He doesn't know how impetuous you are sometimes."

"Impetuous?" I cried, putting my hands

on my hips. "I'm not impetuous! I'm furious! Is it true that you're going to bulldoze Evergreen Forest to put up a lousy industrial park?"

Daddykins looked me in the eye and calmly replied, "Yes."

"But Mr. Lodge," Betty blurted out, "Evergreen Forest is one of the few remaining old-growth forests in the area. You can't destroy it."

"That's right, sir," continued Archie pleadingly. "Those trees can't be replaced in our lifetime. Won't you reconsider? I know you're concerned with ecology and the environment."

It irked me to see that Daddykins was keeping his composure through all of this, while I was about to lose mine. "You all act like I'm doing this out of vengeance or something," he said. "This is just a business deal, and it's one that Riverdale needs and wants. I regret having to destroy that forest, but Riverdale really needs this industrial park. It's going to provide jobs for a lot of people who are now unemployed."

Reggie cleared his throat. "I don't mean to speak out of turn, sir, and no disrespect is intended, but don't you expect to make

a great deal of money out of this?" Leave it to Reggie to get right down to the nitty-gritty.

"Sure I do!" Daddykins answered without a second's hesitation. "That's what big business is all about. Making money isn't a crime, you know."

I glared at my father. "That depends on how you make it," I snapped. "You said Riverdale wants and needs this. It seems to me that only a select few know anything at all about this project." My comment started my friends buzzing behind me. "*We* didn't know anything about it until today."

My father returned my icy gaze. "And since when did you ever take an interest in anything besides boys, clothes, and shopping, Veronica?" he fired back. "You've never had any interest in where the money came from before, as long as there was plenty of it to spend."

My father's cutting words hit home. I did sometimes lead a superficial existence. But it was never too late to change. "You're right, Daddykins," I answered. "But this is one time I have to take a stand—even if it means opposing you."

Daddykins looked at me with concern.

"I'm not trying to make you unhappy. I'd do anything for you. I don't want us to quarrel over this. But this deal is done. There's nothing you or anyone can do to change it."

I heard a collective sigh of dismay behind me. Maybe Daddykins was right, but I refused to budge. Evergreen Forest was too important. I couldn't just let the matter drop. There had to be something I could do.

Slowly I shook my head. "No!" I vowed defiantly. "No. I can't believe all the people in Riverdale would agree to letting that forest be destroyed in the name of so-called progress." I kept shaking my head. "No. I refuse to accept this."

"We Lodges are stubborn, but you're in a no-win situation, Veronica," Daddykins assured me. "I'm going to build that industrial park, and nothing you or anyone else can say or do will stop me."

"I'm not so sure about that!" I responded. I looked at my friends. One by one they all nodded in agreement. Archie looked at me admiringly. It was all the encouragement I needed to continue. I returned my gaze to my father. "Until this question about Evergreen Forest is settled, we're on opposite sides of the fence," I said.

Daddykins shrugged. "It's your decision," he replied. "But it won't matter much. You have only a month before workmen start cutting down those trees."

"A month!" exclaimed Archie. "What can we do in a month?"

"I told you it's—"

"A done deal," Jughead groaned, finishing Mr. Lodge's sentence for him.

"It's not a done deal yet," I said confidently. I hardened my face and stared at my father. "And until Evergreen Forest is saved, you're an enemy! You're my father, but you're the enemy." I turned and led my friends out of the den.

Chapter 4

"Mr. Lodge insists that everyone in Riverdale knows about the project and accepts it with open arms," Jughead said. He paused to take a big bite out of the quarter-pound double cheeseburger he was holding. As he chewed, he looked around Pop Tate's soda shop at the anxious faces of our friends. After we'd left my house, we'd spread the word to all our friends to meet at Pop's later that afternoon. Jug swallowed and then continued. "We have only a month to save Evergreen Forest from the bulldozers."

Big Moose Mason, Riverdale High's star athlete, slammed his clenched fist down on the tabletop. "Duh, Mr. Lodge has no right to wreck our forest," he grunted, getting to his feet. His girlfriend, Midge

Klump, stood up next to him and pushed him back into his chair.

"He does have the right," she said. "It's his forest now. He bought the land fair and square. Didn't you hear Betty say that at the beginning of this meeting?" Midge sat down beside her boyfriend. Moose was an athlete, not an intellectual.

"It doesn't matter who owns the land now," Dilton Doiley said. "It's a question of what the people of Riverdale want done with that land. Originally that property was designated for agricultural use only. It was rezoned for industrial use just recently. If enough people raise a fuss, we might be able to make things sticky for the planning and zoning board and Mr. Lodge."

Dilton shot a questioning look in my direction. I guess he wondered if his talking about my father in that tone bothered me. In fact, a lot of kids suddenly focused their eyes on me. Like it or not, I was the center of attention.

"Dilton's right," I agreed. The truth of the matter was, Dilton was almost always right. He had a genius IQ and didn't tend to make many mistakes.

I stood up. "What we have to do is get

the people of Riverdale to rally to our cause. We've got to make the adults aware of what's going on."

Chuck Clayton and his girlfriend, Nancy, began to clap. Other kids joined in. When the brief burst of applause ceased, I continued. "We've got to spread the word—and fast—if we want to save that forest." I looked at Betty, who was seated next to me.

"That's it in a nutshell," Betty answered without getting up. "But organization is the key. We can't just proceed helter-skelter. If we do, we'll look like a bunch of dopey high school kids who don't know what we're doing."

Everyone nodded in agreement.

"We need someone to take charge. That someone has to be able to stand up to the pressure Mr. Lodge will put on us to quit." Betty looked in my direction. "I think Ronnie Lodge is the person we need to lead us in our campaign to save the forest."

"I agree," Archie said. He began to clap. So did everyone else. Even Jughead put down his cheeseburger long enough to put his hands together a few times.

I looked from face to face in the crowded

room and took a deep breath. "Okay," I agreed. I sat down and everyone moved in closer. The truth was, I was caught a little off guard by what had just happened. In the past I'd planned fashion shows, vacations, parties, and dances, but I'd never taken on anything like this. I was a little bit afraid of goofing things up. I had figured someone like Betty, Dilton, or maybe even Archie would step forward and run the show. Sure, I was angry enough at my father to oppose him, and I certainly wanted to preserve Evergreen Forest. But could I handle this?

It didn't take me long to come up with my answer. If anyone could outlast Hiram Lodge in a duel of wills, it was me. And it was time to prove to Daddykins that I wasn't just a boy-crazy, born-to-shop teenager. With the proper cause to fight for, I could stand up to him. And this cause was worth my best effort.

"Let's get the ball rolling," I started right in. "First we'll need to circulate a petition and hold a public meeting to address the issue of saving Evergreen Forest." I looked at Betty. "You take charge of the petition, Betty," I said. "Organize groups to stand outside of grocery stores and shopping malls—and to go door-to-door."

"Gotcha," Betty replied.

"We should plan on having our first public meeting at the beginning of next week," I continued.

"You can have it right here in my shop," Pop Tate volunteered. He'd been listening attentively from the start. "I don't want to see that forest turned into a bunch of warehouses, either."

"Great, Pop!" Archie exclaimed. He stood up and patted Pop Tate on the back. Reggie whistled. Other kids applauded.

"And I'll be the first one to sign your petition against the industrial park," Pop added. "I didn't know anything about this whole thing until I heard you talk about it today."

Archie looked around. "Did you hear that?" he said. "I'm sure there are many other taxpaying voters who don't know anything about this deal. But they will before we're done." Archie sat down.

"Posters with slogans will help spread the word, too," I said.

"Slogans?" asked Judy Johnson, who had moved to Riverdale not long ago. "Like what?"

"Well, slogans like . . . Evergreen, For-ever Green," I answered, pulling a phrase out of the air. "And I think we should stick with the name Evergreen Forest to give the place increased identity."

"I agree," said Bernadette Brownlee. Bernadette, who sometimes dated Reggie, was the perfect choice to lead the poster-making group. She had a good head on her shoulders and a reputation for getting jobs done. She was a real go-getter.

"Bernadette, you're in charge of slogans and posters," I decided, appointing her to the task. She smiled and nodded her ac-ceptance.

Dilton raised his hand. "We'd better check with the police department to see if we need permits to put up signs and hold meetings," he stated.

"Good thinking," I acknowledged. I looked at Reggie.

"Judy and I will take care of that," he offered. He smiled at Judy flirtatiously. Judy rolled her eyes. She, too, had once dated Reggie but now considered him just a pest.

"You and Jug can handle that," I said to Reggie, much to Judy's relief. "Find out about staging a protest march, too." I

turned to Judy. "Judy can help Bernadette, and so can Midge and Moose."

"Okay by me," Jug said. He started to
attack another burger.

"Great," grumbled Reggie.

"Hey!" cried Dilton. "I know another
way to drum up publicity!"

"How?" I asked.

"Arch and I worked at the local cable-
TV company after school last spring," he
answered.

"So what," muttered Reggie. "If you ask
me, that job was rated PG. And PG stands
for 'pretty goofy.'"

Dilton ignored Reggie and continued.
"While we were there, we worked with
Sandy Randal. She's the woman who
hosts the weekly public-affairs show on
the local channel. It's called 'Good Day,
Riverdale.'" Dilton paused. "I bet Ms.
Randal would agree to have Ronnie on her
show."

"Awesome! That would be totally
great!" Betty exclaimed.

"Do you think she would?" I asked. I
liked the thought of being on television,
even if it was only the local cable channel.

"I'm sure she will," Archie said. "Ms.
Randal is really nice."

"But she'll probably want to air the opposing view, too," Dilton added. He looked at me warily. "You might have to face off against your father on television."

I shrugged. That didn't worry me in the least. "Arrange an appearance, if you can, as soon as possible." I said. Dilton nodded. "Well, that just about does it," I announced. "Check with your group leaders for assignments." I sighed, completely drained. The events of the day had turned the last few hours into a real emotional roller coaster ride.

"You did great," Archie complimented me. He took my hand and squeezed it gently before releasing it. "But you look tired."

"I am," I confessed. Behind us, kids were talking in small groups. "In fact, I'm not sure I'm up for our date tonight," I added, surprising even myself. Archie and I had made plans earlier to take in a movie and then go out for pizza. "Can I have a rain check?"

Archie smiled and nodded. "Sure," he answered. "Anytime. Anyplace. You just name it."

"How about if you pick me up tomorrow morning and we take another drive out to

Evergreen Forest?" I suggested. "Just the two of us. I'll get the cook to pack a little lunch." I chuckled. "And don't breathe a word to Jughead."

Archie snickered. "Okay," he agreed. "But won't that be trespassing? You heard what that man said today."

"How can we trespass?" I replied. "After all, my father owns the land."

Archie nodded. We turned and walked over to talk to the group in charge of the petition.

Chapter 5

My father stared across the table at me as he slowly sipped his morning coffee. I returned his gaze. Daddykins and I were the only ones at the breakfast table. Mother had scheduled an early appointment at the beauty salon and had already left.

"Well?" my father said, lowering his cup from his lips.

"Well, what?" I answered. I started to spread a pat of butter on my toast.

"Well, have you given up that ridiculous notion of trying to save the forest?" he asked.

"For your information, Mr. Lodge," I said, putting my toast down, "my friends and I held a meeting just yesterday to discuss ways to block the development of your silly industrial park." I knew calling my father *Mr. Lodge* and describing his proposal as silly would irk him. It did. For a minute he scowled at me across the table. Then his scowl slowly changed into a broad smile. He laughed out loud.

"That must have been some meeting," he chuckled. "How many chairs did Archie trip over? How many pranks did Reggie pull?" My father grinned. "I hope you held your meeting in a place where Jughead could be well fed. I know how noisy that stomach of his can get when he's hungry."

I stiffened in my chair and glared at my father. "The meeting was held at Pop Tate's," I fired back. "And he's against your project, too!"

Daddykins eased back in his chair and smirked. "Oh, now I'm really worried," he said. He picked up his toast, took a bite, and began to chew.

I gritted my teeth. "Don't be so smug, Daddykins!" I warned. "This whole thing is an explosive issue. It could blow up in your face."

"Veronica," my father said, leaning forward. "I don't understand why you're so opposed to this. It's not like you at all."

I looked my father right in the eye. "Do you think you're the only member of this family who cares anything about the environment?" I asked. "Besides, I have a special attachment to that place." I explained to my father about the walks I used to take when I was lonely.

"I never knew about those walks," my father admitted. "In fact, I never even realized you were lonely when we first moved here."

"That's because you were so busy making money and building on your financial empire that you didn't have much time for me," I said.

My father seemed saddened by my remark. "I apologize for not always being there when you needed me. But I tried my best to be a good father. I can't change the past, and you can't change the fact that that park is going to be built."

"Park! Park! Park!" I cried. "We'll just see if it's going to be built."

"Of course it will be built!" my father answered, raising his voice. "Who's going to stop it—a bunch of teenagers led by bumbling Archie Andrews and my daughter, the queen of shopping sprees?"

I got to my feet and threw my napkin

on the table. "I've just lost my appetite!" I growled.

"Where are you going?" my father called as I walked away.

"To the kitchen," I yelled. "I have to tell the cook to prepare a basket lunch for bumbling Archie Andrews and the queen of shopping sprees. We're going on a picnic today."

"Good," my father said. He picked up his morning paper. "Maybe it'll take your mind off of this park business."

I was waiting near the front door with a picnic basket in my hands when Ol' Betsy announced Archie's arrival by back-firing thunderously. I opened the door and walked toward the driveway.

"Well, you look more rested today," Archie greeted me. He put Ol' Betsy in neutral and leaned over to flip open the door on my side.

"I am," I replied, climbing into the car. I put the picnic basket in the backseat, then settled in beside Archie. "Let's not waste one second of this beautiful summer day." I'd avoided my father since breakfast, and I wanted to keep it that way. A quick getaway was all I asked.

"Right," said Archie. He smiled and put Ol' Betsy into gear. "How did things go with your dad after I dropped you off yesterday?" Archie asked as we headed out of town, toward Evergreen Forest.

"We didn't talk much until this morning," I replied. "And then all we did was have another spat. Daddykins refuses to see our side of this issue." I glanced at the passing countryside. "My father is convinced we've already lost the battle for Evergreen Forest." I paused. "He's so used to getting his own way in business matters that he doesn't feel threatened by anything we might do."

Archie smiled. "Well, I think he's in for a shock this time," he said. "Dilton phoned me this morning. It looks like you're a cinch to get on 'Good Day, Riverdale.'"

"Really?" I squealed in excitement and grabbed Archie's arm.

He nodded. "Mr. Greene, the producer of the show, and Ms. Randal are both coming to our meeting at Pop's soda shop. If the turnout indicates there's a genuine public concern over the park issue, you're guaranteed an appearance on the next show."

I leaned back in my seat. "I sure hope we get a good turnout," I said. "I spoke to Betty and Bernadette on the phone last night. Their groups are moving ahead at a quick pace."

"Reggie and Jug checked procedures at the police department early this morning," Archie told me. "We're all set with permits and things."

Suddenly I felt a bit guilty about driving out to Evergreen Forest for a picnic while everyone else seemed to be working so hard. Archie didn't know it, but there was a secret motive behind this trip. "Maybe we shouldn't be driving out here today," I said.

"Nonsense!" Archie answered. "We're just making up for the date we broke last night. Besides, we can talk about what you're going to say on the TV show over lunch. This trip will be your inspiration."

I nodded. We bounced down the same bumpy, pothole-filled country lane we'd been on the day before. "I think this road is older than some of the trees in the forest," I joked as Ol' Betsy rattled and shook.

Archie laughed and turned onto the dirt road that led to the forest. From there it didn't take us long to reach our destination. We parked in the same place as we had the day before.

"Today *I* lead," I instructed, climbing out. Archie pulled the picnic basket from the backseat and joined me at the edge of the forest. "Come on," I said as I started into the woods. "I want us to picnic someplace special."

"You're in charge," Archie replied. He followed me into the woods. "After all," he added, "this property belongs to you. I'm just a guest here."

"Knock that off," I answered. I blazed a trail through the towering timbers. About fifteen minutes later we reached the place I was looking for. It was a tiny clearing near an old fallen hickory tree. The tree had been struck by lightning many, many years ago. An eight-foot section of the huge trunk still remained rooted in the forest floor, even though it had been lifeless for more than twenty years. That old tree had a special meaning to Archie and me. I wondered if he remembered the place. I looked at him and said, "Let's picnic here. Okay?"

Archie looked around. His eyes came to rest on the tree trunk. He smiled. "Why not?" he said, putting the basket down.

He walked up to the old tree trunk. "If it was good enough for us when we were sixth graders, it should be good enough for us now."

"You remembered!" I rushed up to Archie and hugged him. "Is it still there?" I glanced at the tree trunk.

"Let's find out," he replied, searching the tree for the initials he had carved in the old trunk years ago. "There it is!" Archie pointed at a faded heart, inside which were the initials A. A. and V. L. "I remember that class trip as if it were yesterday," Archie said as we stared at the heart.

"So do I," I answered. I smiled as my mind replayed the memory. Our sixth grade science teacher had taken our class on a field trip. He had brought us out to Evergreen Forest for the day to study the native flora and fauna of Riverdale. Normally I hated field trips, but that one was an exception. The best part of the trip had been when Archie and I sneaked away from Betty and Reggie to have our lunch in private. We had stopped at the old fallen tree, and Archie had carved our initials in the trunk. That was the first moment I suspected I might be in love with

Archie. Seeing him carve our initials that day had kindled a spark of romance inside me that hasn't gone out since. Of course I can't deny it's flickered in the wind a few times over the years, but it still continues to burn. That heart-tattooed tree trunk was another reason why Evergreen Forest was so special to me.

"It sure is quiet out here today," I said, looking deep into Archie's eyes.

"That's because it's Saturday, and there are no workmen in the meadow," Archie replied. He held me tight. Our eyes closed and our faces came close together. Our lips touched as I listened to the sounds of the singing birds. Slowly our lips parted.

"We can't let them destroy this place," I whispered. "We have to preserve it for generations of young people. Everyone should get the chance to make memories here."

Archie nodded. Suddenly we heard the noise of twigs cracking underfoot. The sound of approaching footsteps alarmed us.

"Who can that be?" asked Archie.

We turned toward the noise. Out of the forest stepped a woman, about fifty or so, dressed in the wildest outfit I ever saw.

She had on khaki safari shorts, hiking boots, a safari shirt, and a wide-brimmed hat with feathers stuck in the band. Around her neck hung a pair of binoculars. In one hand she held a walking stick and in the other a black book, and a canteen was slung over her shoulder.

"Greetings!" she called. "Are you nature buffs, plant lovers, or just plain hikers?" She grinned from ear to ear. "I didn't mean to barge in on you, but I was hot on the trail of a round-lobed hepatica—and I seem to have lost it. Have you seen it?"

I glanced at Archie, puzzled. He shrugged. The woman must have detected our confusion because she quickly added, "The round-lobed hepatica is a flower. It has delicate purple petals."

Archie and I shook our heads. "Sorry, we haven't seen any round-lobed hematites," I said.

"That's *hepatica*," the woman corrected, moving closer.

"What are you doing out here?" Archie asked.

"I come out here all the time. I'm president of the Riverdale Horticultural Society, and I'm also a botany professor at Riverdale Community College. Botany is

the study of plants"—she threw that in just in case we weren't familiar with the term. "My name is Professor Helga Kravitz."

Archie introduced us. "I'm Archie Andrews, and this is Veronica Lodge," he said. Professor Kravitz shook hands vigorously with both of us.

"We came out here to have a picnic," I explained.

"This forest is the perfect place for a picnic," Professor Kravitz said. "It's also great for exploring." She leaned close to us confidingly. "Did you know this is the home of a small whorled pogonia, an endangered species?"

"No," I said. "Really?"

Professor Kravitz nodded solemnly. "The orchid needs old-growth forest and blooms only once every few years. We're fortunate to have such a rare flower growing around here."

"Well they won't be growing here much longer if some people get their way," I said sadly.

"What do you mean?" asked the professor.

Archie explained about the industrial park proposal. "Who does that Lodge character think he is?" Professor Kravitz bellowed. Obviously she hadn't made the connection between my last name and his.

"Well, for one thing, he's my father," I said. "But I'm fighting him tooth and nail over this forest!"

"Oh, well, good for you," Professor Kravitz commended me. She reached out and patted me on the shoulder. "I'd like to join forces with you youngsters," she offered. She raised a clenched fist into the air. "I won't stand by and let my beloved nature sanctuary be destroyed. Tell me what my Riverdale Horticultural Society can do to help. We have to save this forest for the pogonias and all the plants."

I smiled. Professor Kravitz would make an impressive ally. "Sit down and have lunch with us," I invited. "We have plenty."

"Delighted," the professor agreed. We all sat down on the picnic blanket.

I looked at our feisty lunch companion. "Would you consider going on television with me to drum up support for preserving Evergreen Forest?" I asked.

"Evergreen Forest," mused the professor. "That's a good name for this place." She glanced around. "And of course I'll go on TV with you. In fact, I'm dynamite on camera. I knocked them dead when I appeared on the 'Flower Power' program two years ago."

"Awesome," I said, reaching for the picnic basket. I winked at Archie. "This trip turned out even better than I expected." I turned to Professor Kravitz. "Welcome to the fight."

Chapter 6

I sneaked a peek at Archie as Professor Kravitz addressed the mass of people crowded into Pop Tate's soda shop for our first public meeting, on Tuesday night. Archie smiled at me. We were both impressed by the massive turnout. People from all walks of life were packed into Pop's place like sardines.

"It looks like the posters Bernadette's group put up generated a lot of interest," Archie whispered. Archie, Betty, Professor Kravitz, and I were seated at a table in the middle of the room. Everyone else was crowded around us. Every chair in the place was taken, and many, many more people were standing. I nodded at Archie. Between the posters, the petitions, and word of mouth, we had stirred up quite a hornet's nest of opposition to my father's proposed park.

As Professor Kravitz continued on about preserving the habitat of the endangered orchid, I checked the faces of our supporters. Professor Kravitz had brought along about thirty members of the Riverdale Horticultural Society, including some important community leaders. The parents of each teenager involved in our movement, except mine, were also on hand, not to mention other assorted relatives. Even Granny Jones, Jughead's eighty-year-old grandmom, was there. Our principal, Mr. Weatherbee, had shown up, and Miss Grundy and Professor Flutesnoot were in the audience, too. Sandy Randal and her producer, Mr. Greene, were seated near Pop Tate. All in all, I'd say we were off to an awesome start.

"And remember," concluded Professor Kravitz, "it is our right as free citizens to determine the growth of our community. Our officials are elected by us to best serve our needs. It is my opinion that a new industrial park may benefit Riverdale's sagging economy now, but at too great a future cost to our environment. Evergreen

Forest must be preserved." She raised a fist into the air. "Evergreen, forever green!" Her closing remarks prompted a burst of enthusiastic applause. I stood up, smoothing out the wrinkles in my skirt. I'd selected my wardrobe for the meeting with great care—I wanted to look attractive, but not flashy, but I'd been unable to resist having my hair and nails done just for the occasion.

"Thank you, Professor Kravitz," I said as the clapping died down. "You've heard about the petition we're circulating, from Betty Cooper, and about the importance of the forest as a plant habitat, from Professor Kravitz. Does anyone else have anything they'd like to say?" I looked around the audience. "This is an informal gathering, so please feel free to express your opinions."

Mr. Andrews, Archie's dad, spoke up. "I have something I'd like to say," he began. "I'm Fred Andrews. Most of you know me. I played in that forest as a kid, as did many of you longtime residents of Riverdale." He paused. "When I first heard about the industrial park months ago, I looked at the proposal only as a businessman. An industrial park would provide new and much-needed revenue for Riverdale. I thought that was good, but I was wrong."

Mr. Andrews looked at me and then at Archie. "My son and his friends have made me realize that some things are more important than money," he continued. "I'd like to see my grandchildren and my great-grandchildren playing in that forest, just like I did."

People applauded. "Fred is right," Jughead's dad called out. "Human beings can make money, but only God can make a tree. I say Evergreen, forever green!" Again there was applause.

Reggie's dad took the floor. "The industrial park would mean more work in Riverdale," he admitted. "Many of us would profit by it. But I'd rather see my company operate in the red for a little while longer than lose a single one of those marvelous old trees."

Reggie whistled through his fingers. "Way to go, Dad!" he cheered.

Betty's mom and dad spoke up next in support of preserving the forest, followed by Miss Grundy and Mr. Weatherbee.

"Not all of the teachers of Riverdale High could be here tonight," Mr. Weatherbee said when he got his chance to address the group. "But Miss Grundy, Professor Flutesnoot, and I conducted a telephone poll and found that more than eighty percent of our teachers and administrators are in favor of fighting to save the forest." That announcement drew another ovation.

When it was quiet again, Mr. Johnson, Judy's dad, raised his hand. I gave him the floor. "I don't want to rain on this parade," he said, "but Miss Lodge asked for opinions, so I'm going to give mine. My daughter dragged me to this meeting." He glanced at Judy. She smiled at her father but seemed a bit uneasy. "I'm not a teacher or a businessman. I'm just an everyday blue-collar worker who moved to Riverdale a short while ago." The crowd grew silent. "The company I was working for went under and now I'm out of work. Things are getting tough. I'd hate to see those trees chopped down, but if it means a new job so I can feed my family, I'll take an ax to them myself." A hush fell over the room. "And I'll bet there are other people here who feel the same way."

"There sure are," Mr. Turner, the father of the Turner twins, called out from the rear of the room. Other voices spoke up in agreement. And although I could never go along with what Judy's dad had said, I admired him for speaking his mind. I certainly could understand his feelings.

"Thank you, Mr. Johnson," I said. Since no one else had anything to say and it was getting late, I thought it best to end the meeting. "We'll be holding another public meeting on Saturday night," I reminded the group. "This time the meeting will be held at the Riverdale High auditorium." I glanced at Mr. Weatherbee. He was the one who had arranged for us to use the auditorium. "I want to thank everyone for coming. Refreshments will be served, compliments of Pop Tate."

People started to move toward the refreshments. Some broke into smaller groups and continued to talk. Betty, Archie, and Professor Kravitz were chatting with me when Dilton walked up with Sandy Randal and her producer, Mr. Greene.

"We're very impressed," Ms. Randal said, congratulating us one by one. "If this keeps up, I'm sure members of the city council and planning board will take notice."

"I hope so," I said.

"We hope Veronica's father will sit up and take notice, too," Professor Kravitz added.

"He already has!"

I recognized my father's voice. He was standing behind us, with Mr. Slattery from the planning board.

"Daddykins!" I exclaimed. "What are you and Mr. Slattery doing here?"

"A wise businessman always scouts his opposition to find out what he's up against," my father replied sternly.

"Hello, Mr. Lodge," said Archie. "Hello, Mr. Slattery."

"I'd like you to meet my father," I announced to the group around me. I made the proper introductions.

"You've got quite a girl here, Mr. Lodge," Professor Kravitz said to my father.

"So I'm finding out," my father answered coolly. "But I think she's going to find out she's fighting a battle she can't possibly win."

"That's right," Mr. Slattery interjected. "You heard what the unemployed gentleman said. Slogans, posters, and meetings won't put food on his table."

"But cutting down an old-growth forest

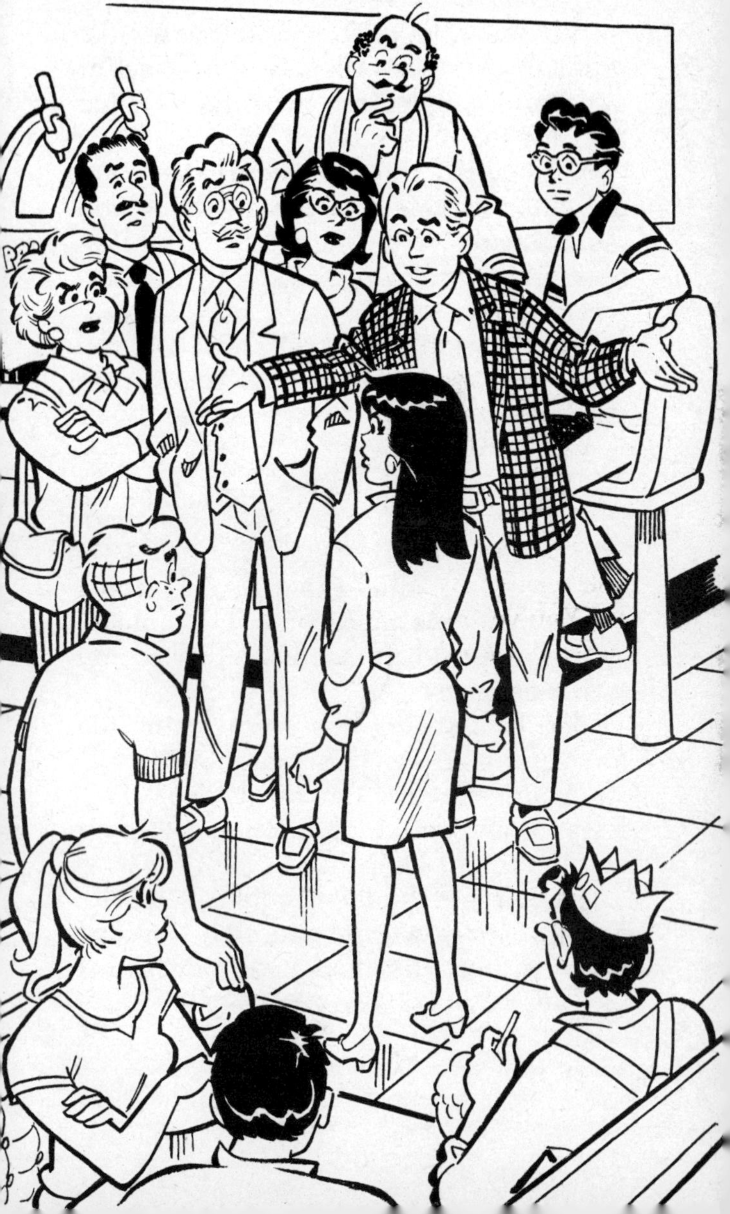

isn't the answer to Riverdale's economic problems," Professor Kravitz fired back at Mr. Slattery. She threw in a dirty look just for good measure.

"Why debate this topic here?" Ms. Randal said, stepping between my father and me. She glanced at Mr. Slattery and Professor Kravitz. "Why not debate it live on local TV Thursday night?"

"That's right," added Mr. Greene. "We'd like to have all four of you discuss the Evergreen Forest issue on the 'Good Day, Riverdale' show."

"What's there to discuss?" Mr. Slattery said. He shrugged. "This is a done deal. We're just here out of curiosity."

A done deal, huh? I thought. If I heard that phrase one more time, I'd explode. "Are you afraid to face us?" I asked my father defiantly.

"You're carrying this enemy thing too far, Veronica," my father cautioned.

"What's the problem, Mr. Lodge?" Professor Kravitz prodded. "You're not afraid of what might happen, are you?"

I saw Archie shudder. Professor Kravitz had thrown down the gauntlet. I peeked at my father. His cheeks were flushed. I knew that look. He was mad—boiling mad.

"Hiram Lodge never backs down from a challenge, madam!" he said curtly. "Slattery and I will be there!" He nodded to Ms. Randal and Mr. Greene. Then he looked at me. "I'll see you at home, young lady." He spun on his heels and headed for the exit, Mr. Slattery in tow.

"When he calls me young lady, it usually means trouble," I told Archie and Betty.

"Are you sorry about all of this now?" Archie asked.

Slowly I shook my head. "Nope. I'm not sorry one bit." I sighed. Inside I just hoped Daddykins wouldn't cut off my allowance or, worse, take away my credit cards. After all, I had to shop for accessories to go with my new dress before my TV appearance on Thursday.

Chapter 7

"Isn't this just so exciting?" my mother gushed as we stood in the studio of the local cable-TV station. All around us, technicians were busily adjusting lights, cameras, and microphone cables. Mother checked my appearance. "You look absolutely stunning, Veronica," she complimented me. "I knew that outfit would look dazzling on you the minute I spotted it in that little Parisian boutique."

I smiled. I'd better look good, I thought, considering all the time it took me to get ready. Wednesday I had gone out and purchased new earrings to match my dress. I had to visit ten stores to find the right ones. Thank goodness Daddykins hadn't revoked my charging privileges. Those earrings had cost a bundle! Then, Thursday, I'd spent most of the day having my hair and nails done. If I didn't look absolutely gorgeous, it wasn't from lack of effort.

"Doesn't Veronica look wonderful?" my mother asked Archie and Dilton. They were standing in the studio, next to my parents and me. We were waiting for Sandy Randal to appear on the set. Professor Kravitz and Mr. Slattery hadn't shown up yet, either.

"She looks totally awesome," Archie agreed, grinning.

"Fabulous," Dilton added, smiling.

Mom turned toward Daddykins, who hadn't spoken more than a word since we'd left the house in our limo. Originally I had planned for Archie to drive me to the studio. However, Mother wouldn't hear of us going in separate cars. She was making a big deal about Daddykins and me appearing on the same TV show together. She even had a special celebration dinner planned for us after the show. I don't think she totally grasped what was going on. She didn't know she was stepping into the middle of a war.

"You look nice, too, Hiram," Mother said to Daddykins. He just grunted in response and adjusted his tie.

"Yeah! You look real spiffy, sir," Archie said, trying to make small talk. Now, Archie was used to being rebuffed by my father. Even in the best of circumstances, they weren't good friends. Still, he wasn't prepared for the chilling look his comment drew from my dad. The smile on Archie's face faded, and he kind of shrank into the shadows.

My father checked his watch. "How long is this thing going to take?" he said, to no one in particular.

Mr. Greene, the producer of the show, overheard my father. He walked up, clutching a clipboard. "We'll be ready to go shortly, Mr. Lodge. We're still waiting for our other guests to arrive."

As if on cue, the studio waiting-room door opened, and in walked Professor Kravitz and Mr. Slattery. They were both dressed for the occasion.

"Greetings, all," called Professor Kravitz as she joined us. "Are we ready to make video history?" My father scowled at her. He seemed much tenser than usual. Daddykins was normally relaxed and confident when he had to speak in public.

"You're late," my father said to Mr.

Slattery. "For a minute I thought I might have to do this alone."

"I got stuck in traffic," Mr. Slattery explained.

"Isn't anyone going to introduce me?" Mother queried. I apologized for my oversight and quickly introduced my mother to Professor Kravitz and Mr. Slattery. She'd already met Mr. Greene.

"I'll get Sandy," Mr. Greene said. "You can all take your places on the set now. It's almost airtime." Mr. Greene pointed at the nearby "Good Day, Riverdale" set.

The set wasn't much more than five chairs arranged around a coffee table, with a "Good Day, Riverdale" logo on a banner behind the chairs. The banner was tacked to tall drapes. A few plastic plants completed the set.

"Mr. Lodge and Mr. Slattery will be in the chairs on the right," pointed out Mr. Greene. "And Veronica, you and Professor Kravitz are on the left." Mr. Greene smiled. "Sandy will sit in the middle and address questions to each of you. Speak in a conversational way and try not to cut each other off. Remember, this is a friendly debate."

"Right," Mr. Slattery said.

"Good luck, everyone," Mother called as we all moved toward the set.

"Thanks," I answered, heading for my chair.

"We're counting on you," Archie said to me. He and Dilton held up their hands and crossed their fingers. I nodded, and Professor Kravitz and I took our seats. I felt a little nervous as the camerapeople before us lined up their shots. I could hear the director's voice coming through the floor manager's headset.

"Switch the monitor on," the director said. "Sandy is on her way into the studio now." The floor manager walked over to a large TV monitor and pressed a power button. Snow flashed on the screen and then an image appeared. For the first time, I saw myself on TV. I smiled. I liked the way I looked.

"Hello again, everyone," Sandy Randal called as she walked up to the set and sat down in the center chair. Suddenly the lights above us went on. The entire area brightened. I squinted a bit. The lights were hot.

Ms. Randal, who was next to me, put her hand on my arm. "Try to ignore the lights," she said. "You'll get used to it." I nodded and sneaked a peek at my father, seated on the other side of Ms. Randal. He still had an angry look on his face.

"Quiet, now," the floor manager called. He held up his hand with all five fingers extended. "We're about to go live." He counted down out loud, dropping fingers as he spoke. After his last finger was down, he pointed at Ms. Randal, who looked directly into the middle of the three cameras focused on us and smiled warmly.

"Welcome to 'Good Day, Riverdale,'" she greeted. "Tonight we're going to hear two sides of an important issue currently causing a great deal of concern in Riverdale. I'm referring to the new industrial park planned for the site now known as Evergreen Forest."

As Ms. Randal continued to set the groundwork for our discussion, I couldn't help peeking at myself in the monitor. I liked the way I looked on TV. I was so busy checking myself out that I didn't hear Ms. Randal introduce us or address her first comment to me. All I picked up was, "Is that correct, Veronica?"

"H-huh?" I sputtered. My cheeks flushed and I squirmed in my seat.

"Let me answer that for Veronica," Professor Kravitz volunteered, coming to my rescue. She leaned over to gaze at Ms. Randal. "How Veronica and her father get along at home has nothing at all to do with this issue."

Professor Kravitz's sharp reply seemed to fluster the host just a bit. "I didn't mean anything by my question," Ms. Randal blurted out. "I just wondered if being on opposite sides of the issue caused any problems for them at home."

"Are we here to gossip about the Lodge family or to talk about the industrial park?" my father interjected.

"We're here to talk about preserving Evergreen Forest," Professor Kravitz called out.

"That forest is past history," Mr. Slattery said. "The park is the future of Riverdale."

"Hogwash and poppycock!" cried Professor Kravitz. She certainly *was* dynamite on TV.

"Ladies! Gentlemen!" called Ms. Randal nervously, holding up her hands to quiet everyone down. Control of the show was rapidly slipping away from her, and try as she might, she couldn't seem to get it back.

"Building that park will wipe out the habitat of a threatened species of owl!" said Professor Kravitz. "Do you call killing off an endangered species *progress*? Do you call murdering trees that have been here longer than Riverdale itself *progress*?"

"That industrial park will provide much-needed jobs and tax revenue for the people of Riverdale," Mr. Slattery yelled back.

"That's right! Make Evergreen Forest suffer for the lack of economic guidance provided by those in power at city hall," Professor Kravitz charged.

"You can't blame our civic leaders for the anemic state of the economy," my father insisted.

"Yes!" gasped a frustrated Ms. Randal. "Who is to blame? Who . . .?"

"Put the blame where it belongs," Professor Kravitz insisted. "The voters will remember this when it's time for the next election. The citizens of Riverdale want Evergreen Forest saved." Professor Kravitz turned and looked directly into the camera. "And if our local politicians want to save their jobs in the future, they'll listen to the voice of the people."

"The people want this park," my father broke in.

I began to sink deep into my seat. I couldn't get a word in edgewise, and I wasn't about to try. Even Ms. Randal, an experienced interviewer, couldn't get her two cents in. The debate had disintegrated into a circus sideshow. I simply tried to melt into the background as the arguing and yelling from both sides persisted. I couldn't wait for the show to end. Finally, after what seemed like an eternal argument, we ran out of time.

"And so . . . and so, if we can get everyone to just shut up for a minute—," Ms. Randal said angrily at the conclusion of the program. I guess she'd finally lost her temper. At last there was silence. Ms. Randal then continued. "We've come to the close of another show." She glared at Mr. Slattery, Professor Kravitz, and my father. She didn't bother to look at me. I had contributed about as much to the discussion as had the plastic plants. "I thank our guests," she said through gritted teeth as the floor manager moved a finger across

his throat in a cutting motion. "Good night! Good-bye! Good day, Riverdale!" The lights dimmed.

"That was a total fiasco!" Ms. Randal screamed, jumping to her feet. "No one will ever watch this show again."

"Are you kidding?" Mr. Greene said, beaming. "The phones have been ringing like crazy. People loved it. I think everyone in Riverdale watched this program tonight."

"Great," grumbled Mr. Slattery as he walked away from the darkened set. My father stormed off the set, too, making his way over to my mother.

Mr. Greene looked at Professor Kravitz. "Professor, you were marvelous," he congratulated her. "You're going to be quite a local celebrity after tonight. We've had at least twenty phone calls from people who thought you were brilliant."

"Thank you," Professor Kravitz said. She turned and winked at me. "I think you can chalk tonight up as a victory for our side."

Archie walked up to me. "Phew!" he said, shaking his head.

"Double phew!" I responded. "Where's Dilton?"

"He sneaked out when the shouting started," Archie answered. "I guess he felt responsible, since he'd helped set this thing up."

I nodded as we walked over to where my mother was waiting. "Where are Daddykins and Mr. Slattery?" I asked her.

"Mr. Slattery bolted out the exit as soon as the show ended, and your father went out to wait in the limo." Mother blinked several times. "Your father is quite upset," she whispered. She glanced at Archie. "I think it would be best if Archie drove you home. It'll give me a chance to calm him down."

"This wasn't my fault," I said.

Mother nodded. "I know," she said, "but if there's one thing your father can't stand, it's being made to look silly in public." Mother giggled a little. "And that Kravitz woman made both him and Mr. Slattery look and sound a bit foolish."

"Gee, I'm sorry," I muttered.

"Don't be," Mother said, patting my shoulder. "Sometimes your father needs to be taken down a peg or two." Mother looked at Archie. "Archie, you'll please stay for dinner when you drive Veronica home," she said warmly. "I planned a special celebration dinner for this evening, and I think you should be part of it."

Archie took a deep breath. "Won't that make things worse?" he asked politely.

"On the contrary," Mother said. "I hope it will help keep the peace between Mr. Lodge and Veronica." She smiled. "Mr. Lodge won't dare explode with a guest at the table—even if it's only you." Mother grinned and walked away.

I took Archie's hand and headed for the exit. "Come on," I said. "We don't want to be late for our dinner engagement with the enemy general."

Chapter 8

I looked across our dining room table, trying to catch Archie's eye. Archie had his head down and was slowly spooning soup into his mouth. I wanted to try to make him feel a bit more at ease, despite the tension-filled atmosphere in the dining room.

"The cook outdid himself with the soup tonight," I said, to no one in particular.

"Yes, it's outstanding," Archie agreed, finally looking up.

"What do you think of the soup, Hiram?" Mother asked. She looked down the table at Daddykins.

"I'd say it was good if I was hungry, but I'm not," he replied gruffly. "And you can tell my daughter for me that she's the reason I've lost my appetite."

"But why don't you tell Veronica yourself?" my mother asked in astonishment.

"I am no longer speaking to her," he answered curtly.

That irked me. "Archie, tell my father I'm no longer speaking to him, either," I said.

Archie's hand jerked nervously, and he accidentally flipped his spoon onto the floor. "Sorry," he apologized. He bent over and retrieved his spoon. When he sat back up, he stared at me pleadingly.

"Tell him," I urged, without looking down the table where my father sat. Archie reluctantly transmitted my message to my father. "And tell him," I added, "that I won't speak to him again until he stops being a defiler of the environment and agrees to stop work on that industrial park that nobody wants."

"Ha!" my father exclaimed before Archie could repeat my words. He tossed his napkin on the table. "*Everyone* wants that park." Obviously, Mother's plan of having Archie stay to dinner so my father wouldn't lose his temper hadn't worked.

"I beg to differ with you, Hiram," Mother said. "A lot of people seem to want that forest preserved. Our phone has been ringing off the hook ever since your appearance on that TV show. And all of the callers seem to agree with Veronica's position." Mother dabbed her lips with her napkin. "Of course, *I'm* neutral," she added.

"So everyone is against me and my industrial park?" Daddykins muttered. "Where were all these defenders of the environment when the planning and zoning board okayed the project? Where will they be when families like the Johnsons and the Turners have to move to a new town, looking for work?" Daddykins crossed his arms belligerently. "Why is everyone against me all of a sudden?"

Archie gulped. He mustered his courage and spoke. "We're not against you, sir, it's just that we're for the environment."

"That's right," I seconded without looking in my father's direction.

"Miss Veronica Lodge is for the environment, is she?" my father grumbled. "If you're so concerned, I suggest that you start walking instead of driving everywhere you want to go. Think of the pollution that creates!" I gulped. Daddykins turned to Archie. "When's the last time you had that jalopy of yours tuned up so as not to smoke so much?"

Archie blinked. "Gee, sir, a tune-up costs money and—"

"Oh, so money is the problem, is it?" Daddykins said. "But making money is evil. It hurts the environment." Daddykins glanced from Archie to me. "If you're going to get up on a soapbox about the environment, I suggest you give it a whole-hearted effort. Start recycling around this town. Instead of letting Smithers and the help do it, get into the kitchen and separate some cans, glass, and plastic yourself."

I stiffened in my seat. I thought about what separating household items would do to my manicure. There was more to being an environmentalist than I'd acknowledged. But though Daddykins was right about most of the things he'd said, he was still wrong about the industrial park.

"I'm not perfect," I said. "Everyone has got to start somewhere. And for me that somewhere is Evergreen Forest."

"Well I'm not perfect, either," Daddykins fumed. "I support many environmental causes, like preserving the rainforest, but I won't back down from building this industrial complex. There's too much money involved, and there are too many jobs at stake." He stood up. "Now if you'll excuse me, I'm going to my den. I'm not in the mood to eat." He stormed out of the room just as Smithers entered.

"Are you ready for the next course, Madam?" Smithers asked my mother. Mother composed herself. Daddy's outburst had shaken her a bit. "Y-yes, Smithers," she replied. "But we'll need only three servings. Mr. Lodge has an upset stomach and won't be finishing the meal."

"Very good," Smithers answered. He left the room.

"Your father is really mad," Archie said to me softly.

"He's going to be even madder next Wednesday, if things go according to plan," I whispered across the table. I was referring to a proposal Professor Kravitz had made the other day. If there was support for the idea at the next public meeting, we would put it into effect bright and early Monday morning. And I was positive that everyone would go along with Professor Kravitz's suggestion.

"What are you two whispering about?"

Mother complained. "Some dinner celebration. First my husband charges out of
here like a wounded buffalo, and now my
daughter is whispering across the table.
What terrible manners."

"We're sorry, Mother," I apologized.
"It's been a difficult day for all of us."

Chapter 9

At 5:00 Wednesday morning we gathered outside Archie Andrews's house. "I can't believe I'm up this early in the morning," I said to Betty, yawning. We watched the guys pack picket signs into the backseat of Ol' Betsy and several other cars. "Do I look okay? Is my makeup on right? I was half asleep when I got dressed and sneaked out of the house."

Betty chuckled. "You look fine," she said. "You're dressed right in style for a protest."

I nodded sleepily. I hadn't realized when everyone agreed to Professor Kravitz's idea of picketing my father's office that I'd have to lose so much sleep to do it. It wasn't that I regretted agreeing to the protest march, it was just that I would have preferred our demonstration take place at a more civilized hour—like maybe high noon.

"Coffee, girls?" Mrs. Andrews asked, walking up to us with a tray of hot coffee.

"No thanks, Mrs. Andrews," I declined. Betty smiled and shook her head, too. "Thanks for letting us meet at your house before the protest," I said.

Mrs. Andrews shrugged. "It's no big deal," she replied. "Mr. Andrews and I decided we should get more actively involved in the fight. Mr. Andrews even took today off from work to participate in this protest."

"We appreciate it," Betty said. "Jughead's and Reggie's dads did the same thing."

I looked around at all the people crowded into the Andrews front lawn. It looked like a lot of people had taken the day off from work. Members of the Riverdale Horticultural Society were present, as were many of our friends and their parents. Teachers from Riverdale High, led by Mr. Weatherbee and Miss Grundy, were also on hand. If I had to guess, I'd say about a hundred people had already assembled. More were expected outside my father's office building in the center of town.

"It's quite a turnout," Mrs. Andrews said.

"Yes," agreed Betty. "Professor Kravitz's TV appearance won us a lot of supporters. Saturday's meeting at the school was standing room only."

Mrs. Andrews looked at me. "I hope this demonstration convinces your father and the Riverdale officials to rethink their position on that park."

"I hope so, too," I replied.

"Well, see you girls at the protest." Mrs. Andrews moved off to circulate through the crowd.

Betty and I started toward several tables set up near the Andrews garage. Boxes of doughnuts and a bowl of punch had been set out for the picketers. "Is everything ready in town for our protest?" I asked Betty. At the public meeting on Saturday, Betty, Dilton, and Dilton's parents had been appointed to procure the necessary legal papers for the demonstration.

"All signed, sealed, and delivered," Betty said. "There will be police on hand to make sure the march goes smoothly. Does your father suspect anything?"

I shook my head. "I'm sure he doesn't," I said. "This will be quite a shock to him. When he drives up to his office building and finds us carrying signs and chanting slogans, it'll blow his mind."

"Hi, Ron! Hi, Betty!" Jughead called. Jug was parked in front of the doughnut table and had a doughnut in each hand. "I never knew being a dissident could be so much fun." He took a bite out of each doughnut and then walked off.

I shook my head. "Sometimes I wonder if you could buy Jughead's allegiance for any cause in exchange for a free meal," I said.

"I don't think so," replied Betty, "but for a banquet, maybe." We both chuckled as Bernadette approached us.

"How are we doing with picket signs?" I asked.

"We should have enough," she said. Bernadette, Betty, and I had spent most of Monday making signs with phrases like Save Our Forest; Evergreen, Forever Green; and my personal favorite, Forests—Not Factories painted on them.

Betty and I headed toward the curb.

Dozens of cars were lined up, waiting to transport protesters and signs to downtown Riverdale. Suddenly Professor Kravitz and Judy came rushing up. From the looks on their faces I knew something was wrong.

"We've got trouble," Professor Kravitz announced.

"Trouble? What kind of trouble?" Archie asked as he joined us.

"It's my dad and Mr. Turner," Judy said. "When they learned about our protest, they decided to do something about it." Judy looked like she was on the verge of tears. "My father isn't usually like this. It's just that being out of work has made him a little crazy."

I stepped close to Judy and put my arm around her. "We understand," I said.

"What happened, exactly?" Archie wanted to know. "The signs are all packed, and we're ready to go. If there's a problem, we'd better get it out in the open right now."

"Mr. Johnson and Mr. Turner have organized a counterdemonstration in support of the proposal," Professor Kravitz responded. "Thanks to Mr. Slattery, they obtained a last-minute permit to march against us. They don't have many supporters, but some of their followers are out of work and might get a little rowdy." She looked at us expressionlessly. "There could be trouble. I don't think there will be, but you never know what will happen at a demonstration like this."

Archie checked his watch. "What do we do? We have to decide right now. If we don't leave in a few minutes, we won't be in time to greet Mr. Lodge when he arrives at work."

Everyone turned to look at me. "It's your decision, Ron," Betty said. "You're our leader. What do you say?"

I hesitated for only an instant. "I say, let's go!" I replied.

"Yahooie!" cried Professor Kravitz. She turned to the crowd. "Let's move out, people!" she shouted. "It's time to picket." She dashed off with Judy.

"See you there," Betty called. She walked off to ride with Reggie.

"Here we go!" Archie said. He took me by the hand and led me toward Ol' Betsy. Before I knew what was happening, I was seated in the front seat of Archie's jalopy, leading a long caravan of cars into downtown Riverdale.

Chapter 10

"Forests, not factories! Forests, not factories!" we chanted as we marched back and forth in front of my father's office building.

"Evergreen, forever green!" I shouted as I waved my picket sign. Archie and Betty were marching beside me. They immediately picked up my chant and repeated it. Up and down the sidewalk we went, waving signs and hollering. It was really something to see.

At the same time, demonstrators protesting our cause marched and yelled just across the street. They were a much smaller group, but they were almost as loud as we were.

"Forests don't feed families!" they shouted as they waved their signs—which weren't as well made or as colorful as

91

ours. "Cut trees, not jobs!" they bellowed as they moved up and down on their side of the narrow two-lane street. All that really separated our two groups was the unbroken yellow line painted down the middle of the road and the six Riverdale policemen on hand to keep the peace.

I looked at my watch. "My father should be here any minute," I told Archie and Betty. "When he sees what's going on in front of his office, he'll freak!"

Archie nodded. "This protest was a good idea," he said. "Look at the publicity we're getting." He pointed at several newspaper reporters who were doing interviews with members of our group. "Professor Kravitz told me that a TV crew from the local affiliate of a major network might even show up."

"That would be radical," Betty said. She glanced at the protesters across the street. "I just wish *they* would go away."

"Don't let them bug you, Betty," Archie said. "As long as they stay on their side of the street, there's nothing to worry about."

"Evergreen, forever green!" I yelled at the top of my lungs. The words were no sooner out of my mouth than I spotted my father's limo approaching. "Here he comes!" I called. I waved to Professor Kravitz in the middle of our protest line. She got the message at once, despite all the racket around us.

"It's Mr. Lodge!" she shouted. "Let's let him know we're here!" She bobbed her protest sign up and down. "Forests, not factories! Forests, not factories!" she screeched, leading the cheer that quickly spread through our ranks.

I was too busy watching the limo's approach to cheer. I saw the car pull over to the curb. I watched as my father opened the door and stepped out, holding his briefcase. I smirked as he whacked his forehead with the palm of his hand in disbelief over the spectacle that greeted him. To his credit, he regained his composure and walked up on the sidewalk. He had started toward the entrance of the building when he spotted me marching with the protesters. We made eye contact just as the trouble started.

"Why don't you tree lovers shut up already?" a man on the other side of the street yelled, stepping into the street.

"Why don't you mind your own business, buster?" someone in our group shouted back.

"Feeding our families *is* our business, punk!" another member of the pro-factory group shouted.

"Drop dead, loudmouth!" a voice answered. I wasn't even sure which side of the street it had come from. I guess it didn't matter. It was the spark that ignited a tense situation. The protesters who wanted the park built suddenly broke ranks and charged across the street. There was a lot of screaming.

"Eek!" I cried as four or five men ran in my direction. I dropped my picket sign and covered my face with my hands. "Daddy!" Somebody shoved somebody else, who ended up knocking me backward toward the landscaped shrubs around my father's building.

"Veronica!" I heard my father yell as I lost my balance and tumbled into the bushes. For a moment I lay there slightly dazed, more from the unexpected turn of events than from the fall itself. I heard shouting, loud screams, and police whistles. I closed my eyes and shook my head. The next thing I knew, Mr. Johnson, Ar-

chie, and my father were all crouched around me.

"Are you okay?" Mr. Johnson asked me. He helped raise me off the wood chips I was lying on.

"Veronica! Veronica! Say something," my father pleaded.

"Are you hurt, Ron?" Archie asked anxiously.

I looked around. Betty and Professor Kravitz were standing there, staring down at me. I smiled up at them.

"I'm fine," I said. "I think I just lost my balance."

"Thank goodness you're okay," my father cried. He took me in his arms and hugged me tightly. "I don't know what I'd do if anything happened to you." In the corner of his eye I saw a tear.

"Don't worry, Daddykins," I reassured him. "I'm fine. Really."

Archie and Mr. Johnson helped me to my feet. I discovered that the ruckus around us had been short-lived. Other than a few pushes and shoves, no damage had been done. No one had been hurt. The police had quickly restored order, and the protest was now over.

"I saw you fall, so I rushed over to help,"

Mr. Johnson told me. "I'm sorry this happened. I wanted to make our feelings about the project public, but I certainly didn't want anyone hurt."

"I know, Mr. Johnson," I said. "I don't blame you."

"I'd better see if anyone else needs any help," Professor Kravitz said, excusing herself. "Who knows? Someone might even want to interview me."

"We'd better help, too," I said to my father. I glanced at Archie and Betty.

"Just a minute," my father said to me. "When you finish down here, come up to my office. And bring your friends with you," he added. "I have something I want to say." He smiled at me and started toward the building.

"He sure was upset when he saw you fall," Archie said.

"He really loves you, Ron," Betty added.

I nodded. "I know," I replied. "I love him, too."

Chapter 11

My father was on the phone when his secretary led my friends and me into his office. It was obvious that she had orders to show us in as soon as we arrived. My father winked at me and held up one finger, indicating he'd be only about a minute more. Reggie, Betty, and Jughead took seats on the huge leather couch. Archie flopped down in a nearby chair. I sat down in the chair closest to the desk. Patiently we waited for my father to finish his call.

"That's right, Mayor," he said. "I know you and the council are upset about what happened in front of my building today. So am I. And I know about the petitions you've received, too." Daddykins spun in his chair so his back was to us. "I think I may have a solution, but I'll have to explore the possibilities a little further. It'll take a few days." He paused. "Yes. That's fine. Scheduling a public meeting on Monday should be okay. I'll keep you posted. Right. Talk to you soon. Bye." Daddykins spun his chair to face us and hung up the phone. He smiled and stood up.

"If the mayor had any hair, he'd be pulling it out over what happened out front today," Daddykins chuckled, jerking his thumb in the direction of the large plate-glass window behind his desk. "Riverdale is a small town. Usually the only protests we see here are on the television at night."

"I guess that means we made history today," I joked.

"That's right," agreed Reggie. "I can see the history books now. They'll read: 'Riverdale's first protest—the shouts heard around the world.'" We all chuckled. Daddykins laughed, too. He adjusted his glasses and then leaned against the top of the desk. "Whatever the fallout from the protest," he said, looking at me, "at least we're talking again."

"That's true," I answered.

"And since we're communicating, I wanted to explain something to you in front of your friends," Daddykins continued, his face softening. "When I saw you

99

fall, I realized how silly this argument between us really is. It's not my business that's important to me—it's you, Veronica." Daddykins paused. "The money I make is for you and your future. Do you understand, Ronnie Doll?"

A chill ran down my body. Ronnie Doll had been my father's pet name for me when I was little. He hadn't called me that in years.

"I think so," I said, nodding slowly.

My father looked at my friends. "I want you all to understand that I'm not some money-grubbing scoundrel out to make a fast buck." Again he looked down at me. "Veronica is used to the finer things in life. I don't mean that in a snobby way. Maybe I've spoiled her, but I want her to continue to have the kind of life she's used to, even after I'm gone." Daddykins turned toward the window. "To do that, I sometimes cut deals that are less than perfect."

Archie glanced at me. "We understand, sir," he said. "What you're saying is that you want Veronica to end up financially secure. I think all parents want their children to be better off than they are, no matter how successful they may be."

"Exactly," Mr. Lodge said.

"But Daddykins," I said as I got up and went over to him. "If making life easy for me means making the world less beautiful or less green, then I'd rather struggle a little." I couldn't believe I had said that. Nevertheless it was true. "Losing something like Evergreen Forest just so I can be comfortable in a mansion someday isn't a trade-off I'm willing to accept." I put my arms around my father. "Evergreen Forest belongs to *all* the people of Riverdale. It's kind of like a savings account for the future of the world. If we hold on to it, it's going to pay big dividends long after we're all gone." I looked into my father's eyes. "I know you're trying to look out for me. But how about the daughters of all the other people in Riverdale?"

"And let's not forget the sons!" Jughead added.

"I *am* thinking about them," my father replied. "I'm thinking about the jobs that the industrial park will provide for men who need work. That park will put food on the tables of people who need it."

I kissed my father on the cheek. "I think I understand all of this a little better now," I said.

"So do we, sir," Archie chimed in, flashing my father a big smile.

"But I still can't stand by and watch you destroy that forest," I said.

"I know," my father replied. "I know. I've been toying with an idea that may solve all of our problems. But I'm not sure it'll work."

"A solution?" I cried excitedly. "What is it? Can the forest be saved?"

"I'm not sure yet," my father replied. "Now get out of here and let me think."

I smiled and pecked him on the cheek. "If anyone can straighten out this mess, you can."

Chapter 12

On Friday night, Archie, Betty, Jug, Reggie, and I were all seated around a table in Pop Tate's soda shop. On the table were three types of pizzas and two pitchers of icy-cold root beer. "Here's to victory!" Jug said. He toasted us by raising a slice of double-anchovy pizza into the air. Jug—and Jug alone—loved double-anchovy pizza.

"It appears that we have the enemy on the run," Reggie added, raising a glass filled with root beer.

"To victory," Archie cried. He saluted with a slice of sausage pizza.

"Hold on," I cautioned. "The battle isn't over yet. Let's not get too confident. No one has said the industrial park isn't going to be built."

"Leave it to Ronnie to spoil a victory

celebration with minor details," Reggie grumbled. "The mayor and the city council called for a special public hearing about the complex on Monday. They're going to throw in the towel. Just you wait and see."

"I agree with Ronnie," Betty put in. "Just because Professor Kravitz called a truce until after Monday's meeting doesn't mean we still won't have to fight for Evergreen Forest."

"That's right," I said. "Let's not celebrate prematurely. We can't be sure what the council or, for that matter, my father, will do."

Archie put down the slice of pizza he was nibbling on. "Hasn't your father given you a clue as to the solution he's working on?"

I shook my head. "My father has been so busy meeting with his corps of engineers that I've hardly even seen him for the last two days. I haven't a clue to what he has in mind," I admitted. "All I know for sure is that he hasn't given up on that project just yet."

"But what if the town officials order him to stop construction?" Reggie asked. "He'll have to give in then."

Again I shook my head. "Let's remember that money talks, Reggie," I reminded him. "My father does own the land. If the town tries to go back on its agreement, my father could fight it in court, and his corporation can afford the best legal minds in the country."

Reggie gulped. "Then your father is still our enemy," he remarked. Reggie's words cut through my heart like a knife. I thought back to the look on my father's face when I'd fallen during the protest march. I recalled the tears in his eyes and the way he'd hugged me. I remembered the talk in his office, the way he'd called me Ronnie Doll.

"No, Reggie," I said. "My father is not our enemy. He might not agree with us, but he's trying to do what he thinks is best for everyone involved. He's not our enemy, and he's not Riverdale's enemy."

I sighed. Most of all, I realized he wasn't *my* enemy. I regretted ever saying that to my father. We'd just about patched up our feud, but I still hadn't apologized to him for calling him my enemy or told him how much I loved him. We might have differences of opinion, we might argue and fuss and fight over things big and small, but we could never really be enemies. I knew that now. Suddenly I felt very weary.

"Archie," I said. "Could you drive me home? I'm feeling kind of tired."

"Sure, Ron," Archie agreed. "No problem."

"The celebration can't be breaking up already," groaned Jug. He grabbed another slice of pizza. "I just started to have fun."

"Think of it this way," Archie told Jug. "With us gone now, there'll be more pizza for you to finish up." Jug glanced at the two other—mostly uneaten—pies on the table before him. His eyes lit up like Christmas lights.

"Go figure," I heard Reggie say as Archie and I headed toward the door. "First Mr. Lodge is our enemy, and now he isn't. Go figure."

"Reggie never was too bright," Archie whispered to me as he held open the door. We walked out into the night and strolled over to the curb where Ol' Betsy was parked. We climbed in and Archie turned the key. *Ka-pow!* Ol' Betsy's motor began to purr like a contented kitten.

"She sure runs great since I had her

tuned up," Archie said. He patted the dashboard with his hand.

I smiled. My father's comment at the dinner table had really made Archie think.

Even though it was a beautiful summer evening, perfect for romance, I couldn't wait to get home. I was hoping my father would be there. I wanted to smooth out all the rough edges between us before another night passed.

"You're sure not much for conversation tonight," Archie said as we approached the main gate of the Lodge estate. "You haven't said a word since we left Pop Tate's."

"Sorry, Archie," I apologized as Ol' Betsy stopped in front of my house. "I guess I have things on my mind."

Archie was going to walk me to the door, but I told him he didn't have to. I gave him a short but sweet good-night kiss and then hopped out of the car.

"Bye, Ron," Archie called.

"Bye!" I went into the house and found Mother standing in the foyer. "Where's Daddykins?" I asked.

"He's supposed to be going with me to the Ladies Auxiliary dinner at the country club," Mother grumbled. "But he's barricaded himself in his den with a bunch of blueprints and plans." She exhaled loudly. "I'll never forgive him for canceling out on me at the last minute like this."

I smiled at Mother. "Yes you will," I predicted. "Daddykins isn't the kind of person you can stay mad at for long." I started toward my father's den.

"What a family," Mother mumbled. "One day she's not speaking to her father, and the next she's sticking up for him."

"Bye, Mother," I called. "Have a good time."

"I'll have a terrible time," Mother replied. "But at least I won't be the only woman there without an escort. Mr. Wadsworth and Mr. Turnbull never go to these dinners, either."

I chuckled. Then I walked up to the den door and lightly rapped on the wood.

"Yes," my father called.

I opened the door and peered in. Daddykins was behind his desk, his nose buried in a mountain of papers and plans.

"Oh, hello, Veronica," he said as he adjusted his glasses.

"I can see you're busy, so I won't take up much of your time," I said.

"I always have time for my favorite

daughter," he replied, "though I have to get a number of things sorted out in time for Monday. In fact," he continued, "I have special meetings scheduled with my engineers all weekend."

"I just wanted to tell you something," I said. "A little while ago I called you my enemy because of this forest issue. That's not true. You're not my enemy. You're my friend." I shrugged. "It may sound silly, but it's important to me."

"It's important to me, too," Daddykins replied. "Thanks for telling me."

I smiled. I felt much better. "I love you, Daddykins." I started to leave.

"I love you, too," my father answered as he returned his gaze to the blueprints before him. I went out, leaving him to his work.

Chapter 13

The meeting hall of the Riverdale Municipal Building buzzed in excitement on Monday night. The huge room was overflowing with people all there for one reason: to discuss the Evergreen Forest–Industrial Park issue. Professor Kravitz and her bird-watchers group were seated in a section near my friends and me. Mr. and Mrs. Andrews and other parents were scattered here and there in the crowd. Mr. Weatherbee, Miss Grundy, and a mob of teachers were also present, as were Mr. Johnson and supporters of the proposed complex. Archie, Betty, Jug, Reggie and I had arrived early and had front-row seats. Behind us was clustered our action group—Bernadette, Dilton, Midge, Moose, and Nancy.

"It looks like everyone in town is here,"

Archie whispered to me as we waited for the meeting to be called to order. I looked up at the stage where Riverdale's mayor and council members were seated. Mr. Slattery of the planning board was there, too.

"Not everyone is here yet," I replied. My father was noticeably absent from the proceedings.

"Your dad *is* coming, isn't he?" Betty asked me.

"I'm sure he is," I answered. I wondered where my father could be. Behind us the crowd was getting restless. The meeting had been scheduled to begin at seven o'clock and it was now ten past. I looked toward the stage. Mayor Higgins was fidgeting in his chair. Beads of sweat were pouring off his bald head. As the crowd got more noisy, Mayor Higgins nervously got to his feet and approached the microphone on the podium. He cleared his throat and pulled a handkerchief out and mopped his brow.

"Ah, good evening, everyone," he greeted. "For those of you who don't know me, I'm Mayor Higgins. We've scheduled this informal public meeting tonight to discuss a topic of recent concern. I'm referring to the industrial complex H. L. International Development Corporation plans to build on the former public land site known now as Evergreen Forest."

Mayor Higgins gulped and glanced at the council members on the stage. A slight groan of discontent rose from the audience. "To explain the proposal further," Mayor Higgins continued, "I turn the microphone over to the head of the planning board, Mr. Slattery." A few people applauded politely, but for the most part the room was ominously silent. Mr. Slattery wasn't a very popular man at the moment.

"As you all know, plans for the industrial complex have already been drawn up and approved." That comment drew a resounding chorus of boos from the crowd. My friends and I joined in to add our boos to the ballyhoo. When the crowd quieted, Mr. Slattery continued, unflustered by the din.

"However," he said, "Mr. Hiram Lodge, the chairman of the board of H. L. International Development Corporation, has informed me that he has some drastic changes to unveil at tonight's meeting." Hearing that, the demeanor of the crowd seemed to improve instantly. "The problem is . . ." said Mr. Slattery, "Mr. Lodge has not arrived at the meeting yet." Again the temperament of the crowd shifted, this time from good to bad.

"Well, where is Lodge?" someone on the far side of the room yelled out.

"Be patient," said Mr. Slattery. "I'm sure he'll be here any—"

Suddenly a voice boomed out from the rear entrance into the hall. "I'm here now!" With three engineers loaded down with blueprints and plans trailing behind him, my father moved rapidly up the middle aisle of the room and toward the podium.

Mr. Slattery smiled. He leaned close to the mike and said, "I now turn this meeting over to Mr. Hiram Lodge." Then he returned to his seat.

My father was greeted by a few scattered boos as he prepared to talk. His engineers lined up behind him. "When you plan to build something like this industrial park," he announced, "you can't always please everyone." He paused and looked out over the now-silent crowd. He spotted me and my friends and gave us a wink and a nod. I smiled and wiggled my fingers in a half wave.

"Some people want the park," he stated. "Some people want to keep the forest." His stern expression softened. "Well, after some hard work and a few radical revisions, I can now present a plan to Riverdale that calls for the building of a smaller industrial complex that will still preserve most of Evergreen Forest."

My father paused. "A slightly smaller complex will still give Riverdale the jobs and revenue it so desperately needs," my father said. "At the same time, it will allow for the old-growth section of Evergreen Forest to remain intact forever, as public land donated by H. L. International Development Corporation to the people of Riverdale and their descendants."

A thunderous shout of approval arose from the crowd. "Hooray for Hiram Lodge!" I heard someone yell. I turned and saw Professor Kravitz cheering my father. Tears formed in my eyes. People applauded wildly as my father waved his hands to calm the crowd. When the noise died down, he continued.

"Thank you," my father said, acknowledging the accolades of his audience. "But of course the council and planning board will have to okay the new plans before they can become official." He turned toward his engineers and motioned to them. They distributed the stacks of papers they were holding to everyone onstage. Before he even received his set of plans, Mr. Slattery got up and returned to the microphone. My father stepped aside.

"I think I can speak for the council and the planning board when I say that unless these plans are completely off base, we'll eagerly and speedily approve them." Mr. Slattery smiled and shook hands with my father. For the first time that evening, Mr. Slattery got a big hand.

My father returned to the mike. "Since that's the case," he began, "I have something I'd like to add. At first I didn't think Evergreen Forest could be saved. Someone inspired me to rethink my original plans, to make some adjustments with the preservation of the environment in mind." My father looked at me. "That person was my daughter Veronica. Without her, this new project would not have been possible."

Everyone clapped as I got to my feet and bowed politely. Once more, tears formed in my eyes. I'd never felt so proud of myself and my father in my life.

Chapter 14

"Now *this* is what I call a celebration," my mother said, "even if it was planned on such short notice."

My mother had managed to conjure up a dinner party in my father's honor and mine in just one day's time. Usually it took her a month to plan something as simple as lunch for friends. "You did a wonderful job, Mother," I complimented her.

I looked around the table. Seated near my father were Mr. Slattery, Mayor Higgins, and their wives. Also at the table were Archie, Betty, Jug, Reggie, Dilton, Midge, Moose, and Bernadette. Last but not least, seated right next to Mother, was Professor Kravitz, all decked out in her best dress.

"Your choice for the menu was simply inspired," my father said, lifting a glass to toast my mother's effort.

"It sure was, Mrs. Lodge," Jughead agreed. "It's seldom that I get to enjoy such a delicious meal on a Tuesday night."

"Oh?" said Mother. "And why is that, Jughead?"

"Tuesday is the night we always have leftovers at my house," Jughead explained.

"I didn't think you ever had any leftovers at your house," Reggie wisecracked.

We all chuckled.

"Now don't forget, Professor," Mother said to Professor Kravitz when the laughter had died down. "You're going to provide me with information about your bird-watchers club."

"It will be my pleasure, Mrs. Lodge," the professor answered. "Now that we know Evergreen Forest will be here forever, we expect to attract a lot of new members." She glanced at my father.

I looked down the table. "A toast to the man who saved Evergreen Forest," I proposed, lifting my glass. The other guests lifted their glasses, too. "Here's to my father," I said. "A business wizard—and a true environmentalist." I paused a second and then added, "Here's to Hiram Lodge, my father and my friend!"